HAPPILY EVER AFTERED

A HAPPY CAT NOVELLA

PIPPA GRANT

LILI VALENTE

1

Colin Bassingstoke, aka a man very much out of his element

THE ONLY THING WORSE THAN BELATEDLY REALIZING you're in love with a woman?

Realizing you may have already lost her.

Forever.

Although, having your ten-year-old daughter handed a biscuit in the shape of a phallus while attempting to locate the love of your life is also near the top of the list of *worst things that can happen to a man.*

"No biscuits before lunch," I tell Beatrice, covering the confection with my handkerchief and whisking it from her view. "Have you seen Savannah?"

The question is mostly to distract her from the fact that I've just snatched sugar out of her hand. The only thing my daughter loves more than playing Ninja Rabbits with Rabies—a game she and Savannah invented when she was younger—is scoring a forbidden sugary treat.

I try to keep her away from sugar and, quite honestly, places like this one.

This town, so far, is proving to be every bit as insane as I expected from listening to Savannah's stories.

Happy Cat has its charms—a fine town square with some interesting architecture and a lovely river we spotted on the way in from the airport—but the towns-folk seem a bit unhinged. Beatrice and I are currently surrounded by locals buzzing about a game of Dildo Football the sophomore girls are playing later tonight and the *annual treasure hunt for love* about to get under-way. I didn't realize love was something that could be hunted, but apparently it is. And the townsfolk seem eager to participate, either in the hunt or in the cheering.

The crowd does finally appear to be thinning a bit, but if Savannah is here, thus far I've been unable to locate her.

"Papa, we shouldn't be ashamed of our body parts," Beatrice chides me as she attempts to recover the biscuit. "I've eaten biscuits shaped like hearts and noses before. I see no difference at all with eating *this* biscuit."

"The difference is not giving your father heart palpi-tations, love. Come. We have more important things on our agenda."

"Papa!" She grabs my biscuit-free hand and squeezes it tight. "Is that George Cooney?"

Both a raccoon and the woman holding its leash

turn and peer at us as Bea points a finger their way. The woman smiles, and my heart pitter-patters like Beatrice's feet did once upon a time in our London flat when she was small.

I've never been to this part of the world before, but I feel as though I know it and its inhabitants quite well. "Cassie?" I ask. "Cassie O'Dell?"

She tilts her head. Her brow furrows slightly above her spectacles, but her smile remains. "Yes. I'm sorry, have we met?"

Beatrice drops my hand and charges the poor woman as though they've been separated from birth. "You're Cassie! Savannah keeps your picture on her nightstand. Where are the babies? And the rest of George's family? We don't have raccoons in England. Oh, they're even cuter in real life than in pictures!"

"Beatrice?" Cassie gasps.

"Yes!" My daughter hurls herself into the woman's arms, hugging her so tightly that Cassie's eyeballs bulge a little. "So happy to meet you!"

"Oh my goodness, me too. You look exactly like your picture, but I didn't expect to see you *here*." Her bulging eyes shift in my direction. "So you must be the mysterious Mr. Bassingstoke, AKA Savannah's boss?"

I clear my throat while the raccoon plops back on his haunches and studies me with a skeptical look, as though judging whether or not I'm worthy of talking to his mistress. "Yes. Call me Colin, please. How do you do?"

"Where's Savannah?" Beatrice asks as she crouches

down to extend a hand toward the raccoon. To my relief, the creature seems instantly smitten with Bea and submits to her gentle strokes along its fur with good temper. She pets it with a look of wonder that makes me silently promise to take her with me on trips more often. "Papa finally realized he has to tell Savannah how important she is to us, but it might be too late. She already ran away. We really want her back though."

My cheeks grow warm.

Waking up to find Savannah gone yesterday, with her letter of resignation resting on the desk in my study, was the wake-up call I needed to admit what I've been denying for far too long.

It's a cliché to fall madly in love with the nanny, but after three years, I can no longer deny my feelings.

I can, however, understand why it took this long to come to my senses.

The first year with Savannah was, frankly, rather wretched. Her fanciful notions and habit of sneaking Beatrice ice cream against my express orders that sugar only be allowed on Saturdays annoyed me endlessly. But she was the first nanny to stick around for more than two weeks since Beatrice's mother passed away— allegedly the others found my home "cold"—thus I held my tongue, taking comfort in the fact that Bea and Savannah got on so well. By the second year, Van's whimsical nature had become a normal part of life, but it never occurred to me as I re-entered the dating world that the woman I was looking for was right in front of me the entire time.

This past year, though, it's become obvious there's more to our relationship than a boss and his employee or even two friends. I'm finding it increasingly hard to fight my attraction to this gold-hearted, free-spirited, selfless being who's brought such joy and sunshine into our lives. And maybe I *wouldn't* have fought it if I hadn't been afraid I'd muck things up with Savannah the way I have with every other woman I've dated. Or if I hadn't also been afraid that Beatrice would end up losing the most important person in her life.

I am under no delusions that *I'm* that person.

I love Beatrice with all my heart, but I work sixty hours a week and have no talent for whimsy or playing pretend. I know I'll always be her papa and loved because of it, but I'm no Savannah. I don't light up a room—or a little girl's heart—when I walk into it.

So, I've done my best not to cross the line between friendship and something more.

And then, less than a month ago, I found Savannah balancing on the countertop in the kitchen, reaching for a bowl stored high in the cabinets. I shouted at her for not fetching the stepladder, asking if she wanted a broken neck. She yelled back that "Yes, I've been dying to have a broken neck for years, Colin. And now I'm about to make my dreams come true. Go away and let me make cookies. Thursdays are also an excellent day to eat sugar."

I, however, did not go away. I fetched the stepladder, then the bowl, then Savannah off the counter. As I guided her feet back to the floor with my hands around her waist, our bodies brushed together in a way they hadn't before. My pulse quickened, longing roared in my chest, and it took every bit of my considerable willpower to resist the overwhelming urge to kiss her.

Her breath rushed out, and her lips parted, but I was afraid to believe in the desire I saw reflected in her gaze. I convinced myself I must be imagining things. She's young and vibrant and beautiful, and I'm a "stuffy stick in the mud," as she's told me many times, usually when I'm refusing to run barefoot through the daffodils at Hyde Park with her and Beatrice.

And supposing she *did* feel even a little of what I felt, the fact remained that propositioning an employee isn't seemly behavior for a barrister or anyone else. As long as she's in my house, under my roof, caring for my daughter—and for me, by extension—it would be improper to ask for more. I convinced myself I could refrain from acting on my feelings until Beatrice was of an age when it would feel appropriate to ask Savannah to join me for dinner or on a business trip. Or in my bed.

That I could maintain the status quo for another six or seven years, or however long it took to feel strong enough to survive it if she rejected me.

But her letter of resignation yesterday made it clear that I'd waited too long.

Dear Colin,

I'm so sorry to go like this, but the

truth is I was afraid if I said "goodbye" face to face I might never leave. I've grown so attached to both you and Beatrice that I've lost touch with my own hopes and dreams. And while a part of me would be overjoyed to spend another three years as Bea's nanny, another part of me knows it's time to stop hiding in someone else's life and go find my own.

It's time for me to move on to the next adventure.

Please give Beatrice all of my love and promise her that I'll never forget my favorite person in the entire universe. And that I'll be sure to write her a nice long letter as soon as I'm settled.

With appreciation and affection,

Van

Cassie, Savannah's sister, is studying me with the perceptiveness of a woman who knows the answers to all of the questions I can't seem to force myself to ask.

"Van just left for the treasure hunt." She points to a large sign hung from the posts of the picnic shelter. A giant sun is making quite the ecstatic face above the words *Sunshine Toys is This Year's Sponsor of…Happy*

Cat's Spring Treasure Hunt for Love! "We love our fun around here."

"A treasure hunt!" Beatrice cries, standing so abruptly the raccoon tumbles over as she removes her hand from his scruff. "Oh, sorry, George. But we have to go find Savannah. Come on, Papa, let's go sign up now! Before it's too late! We can help her win, and then she'll be so happy she'll forgive you for being grouchy."

Cassie makes an awkward noise, and while I might be incredibly slow on the uptake when it comes to recognizing that I'm in love, I'm well aware that Savannah ran an adult product company before coming to England following her divorce and that this event is now sponsored by the same.

Which means I'm guessing my daughter should *not* participate in this treasure hunt unless I'm ready to have an in-depth discussion of sex toys. All discussions with Beatrice are in-depth. My daughter is like a starved dog after a bone when it comes to acquiring information, especially information I'd rather not share until she's older.

We survived the puberty discussions—all credit to Savannah—but I'm not ready for the adult novelty products or *ehem* "self-pleasure" discussion just yet.

"I don't think that's a good idea, darling," I say.

"Why not?" Beatrice demands, propping her hands on her hips.

"I need to speak with Savannah immediately," I tell Cassie. "Do you think—"

"And you couldn't just call her?" Cassie cuts in.

"Of course not," Beatrice answers for me. "Like Savannah always says, begging for forgiveness is something that should be done face-to-face. That's why she made me go over to Mean Molly McKibbon's to apologize after I put frogs in her dress pockets at the park." Bea holds up a hand to her mouth as she adds in a faux whisper, "Even though Molly deserved frogs in her pockets because she always cheats at games and cheaters are the worst."

"They really are." Cassie nods solemnly, but her eyes are twinkling as she turns back to me. "You didn't hear this from me, but the first clue leads to the fire station. If you'd like, Beatrice could come home with George and me, then you and Savannah can swing by my place when you're finished with your discussion. I mean, if that's okay with you. I'm trustworthy, I promise, and George hasn't snuck out of the house to dumpster dive in ages."

The raccoon on the leash nods at me, as though he, too, has read between the lines and agrees that I'll move quicker if I'm by myself and that navigating a sex toy treasure hunt is something I should do *without* my daughter's assistance.

And it's not like Cassie's a complete stranger. After all the stories Savannah has shared about her sister, I know her better than most of my own family members.

"That way Beatrice could meet George's kiddos and our new kitten, Lucifer, who is, I'm pretty sure, the cutest kitten in the entire world."

"Oh, yes, please, Papa!" Beatrice clasps her hands

together at her chest. "I really want to see Savannah, but I *don't* want to miss the raccoons or the kitten."

"All right," I say, "but be on your best behavior for Cassie." Glancing up at Cassie, I add, "Thank you so much. I appreciate your help."

"Of course," she says, a knowing look in her eyes. "Good luck. I have a feeling you might need it."

2

Savannah Sunderwell, aka a woman determined to give love one last chance

THERE'S NOTHING LIKE BEING THE FIRST TREASURE HUNTER to reach the second clue *and* getting a giant bear hug from your favorite brother-in-law to banish a bad case of jet lag.

Cassie really won the hubby lottery when she married Ryan.

"Savannah!" He gives me one last squeeze before setting me back on the ground. "Cassie just texted that you were back in town. When did this happen?"

He's in a Happy Cat Fire Department tee shirt and work pants, and he's not alone. My nephew, Logan, an adorable, chubby-cheeked toddler with two fingers in his mouth, a fire truck on his shirt, and wide brown eyes, is peeking at me from beside a table holding coolers of punch and stacks of cups for the treasure hunt participants.

My heart squeezes.

I wave at him and smile, but he shrinks back.

My heart aches, but I know his shyness isn't personal. He just needs to warm up to me again. The last time I saw him, he wasn't even crawling, and now he's walking and growing up way too fast. I'm missing all of his little guy years, and I can't miss watching Logan grow up, because…

Well, because he could be the only baby I ever see grow up.

I don't want to be envious of my sister and her family—I'm so happy that they have each other—but lately I've been forced to come to terms with the fact that I might never have a family of my own.

And it's not just the challenge of finding a man who loves me and wants to raise a baby together—which is no easy feat in the dating-app-fueled shit show modern courting has become. It's also the news from my doctor last week that I'll never be able to carry a baby of my own. My endometriosis has left too much scar tissue behind for my ovaries to function properly. Surrogacy is on the table, but I can't bear to think about it yet. I'm still mourning the news that my body has betrayed me.

Plus, I'm not ready to become a single mom. I still have dreams of doing the whole family thing the old-fashioned way, with love and marriage *before* the baby carriage.

When Cassie reminded me that the treasure hunt for love was this weekend—right after I'd spent yet another night watching a movie inches away from Colin on the couch and lamenting the fact that he barely looked at me the entire time, let alone seemed to feel the sexual tension humming between us the way I did—it felt like a sign.

It was time to come home.

It doesn't matter that Colin's the only man I can think about or that Beatrice feels like my daughter in many ways. They're *not* my family. I'm an employee, nothing more, and Colin could decide to let me go any day now. Beatrice is nearly eleven, after all, and so busy with after-school activities that she doesn't really need a full-time nanny anymore.

As much as it hurt to admit it, my life in London was becoming another dead end, just like after my divorce. But this time, instead of being filled with right-eous anger at my cheating husband and his deplorable behavior with that sheep, I'm just sad.

There's nothing wrong with Colin. Yes, he's stuffy and grumpy and almost ridiculously British, but those things don't bother me as much as they did in the beginning. He may be stuffy, but he has a secret soft side, loves his daughter to the moon and back, and has never treated me with anything but kindness and respect, even in the early days when I could tell he thought my tendency to roll around in the grass with Beatrice at the park was undignified.

God, I wish I was in the park with her right now. I

miss her so much it's like someone removed a vital organ while I was napping on the plane.

"I flew in yesterday but stayed at a hotel near the airport since I got in late," I tell Ryan, forcing my thoughts back to the here and now. My life in Britain is over. It's time to hurl myself into my new life, no matter how shell-shocked I still feel. "I've been missing you all so much. And I had a long call with Olivia earlier this week, and I just… I realized it was time to come home."

His brows shoot up his forehead. "Oh, wow. So you're home for good?"

I try to smile but fail. Ugh, I'm so tired of failing. "Yeah. Well, for a while, at least. We'll see if the wind decides to blow me somewhere else eventually." I clear my throat and wave a hand at my face, blinking as tears make the back of my nose sting. "Goodness, I forgot how bad my allergies are here in the spring." I sniff hard, willing myself to pull it together as I clap my hands. "Now, back to the drama at hand—where's my next clue? I don't want to miss another moment of the Happy Cat fun."

And I want to land the true love prize at the end of this treasure hunt rainbow. According to town legend, the winner of the treasure hunt always meets his or her perfect match within a year of landing first prize.

I want to believe magic like that is possible and that a year from now I might be over Colin and happy with a good man of my own.

I wince, my lizard brain not liking the thought of

ending up with any man but Colin, but my lizard brain is stupid. It's a primal ball of dumb that can't be allowed to call the shots. It's a gecko that's had one too many brushes with death to be trusted to lead the gecko pack anymore, and I need to move on without it and learn to trust my inner elephant instead. Beatrice wrote a paper on elephants last year, and they're such smart animals. I have to trust that my inner elephant will convince me that Colin is the past and the mysterious Mr. X is my future—assuming I win first place.

And if I want to win, I need to get that next clue. The laughter outside suggests the other singles in town aren't far behind me.

I wave an urgent hand at Ryan. "Come on, brother, give me the goods."

"I can't, not even for my favorite sister-in-law," he says with a laugh, "but I am allowed to advise all hunters that the next clue isn't located on the fire truck or inside the station. It's hidden somewhere a little more…trashy."

He casts a pointed glance toward the back door, and I'm off with a soft "thank you!" tossed over my shoulder.

I dash away just as a group of older ladies wearing matching "Mama Wants Some Lovin'" tee shirts step through the open garage door. Luckily, they're distracted by the hunky cuteness of Ryan and the baby cuteness of my adorable nephew, and I'm through the door before any of them notice me.

Out back, I hurry past the lawn chairs circled around the fire pit and the two massive barbeques the fire station puts to use for family meals and fundraisers and make a beeline for the dumpster at the edge of the graveled area. I find the small folder full of identical clues taped to the back almost immediately and for a moment consider reading one and tossing the rest of the clues into the dumpster to throw the other hunters off the trail.

But I can't. Cheating isn't me. I've suffered for other people cheating, and I've watched people I love get hurt by cheating. I can also hear Olivia in both my lizard head and in my elephant heart, reminding me that cheating and foul play cast ugly shadows over this beautiful earth we've been given. Prizes—especially magical ones—require fair play.

Besides, there's nothing Beatrice hates more than a cheater, and I love her too much to let her down, even if she'll never find out about it.

So, I grab a single clue and skim it quickly.

It's a great day for a song or a dance. Squint into the bright lights when you get your chance. Pro tip: Love songs are sure to turn a gray sky blue, but watch out or you might catch a buzz before you find this next clue.

Oh! I know this one!

I hope.

I think.

How much has Happy Cat changed since I've been gone?

Surely not much. And even if there are other places in town now where a person might "catch a buzz," I'm positive none of them have karaoke except The Wild Hog. And "squint into the bright light when you get your chance" must mean we all have to perform a song to get our next clue.

A wave of sadness momentarily hits me again as another unbidden memory pops into my head. Colin's office had a family holiday party last year, and since he worked so late that day, I had to take Beatrice to meet him. When I got there, he invited me to stay, and how could I resist my stiff and proper but oh-so-irresistible boss handing me a hot buttered rum?

I couldn't.

And as I hovered near the back, I watched Beatrice convince him to sing karaoke with her.

When Mr. Stuffy took the stage to perform a horribly awkward version of "All I Want For Christmas Is You" with his daughter and the amazing voice I didn't realize he had, I knew I was well and truly in love.

I shake off the memory. It's time to move. If I'm the first person to sing for my next clue, I'll have at least a two- or three-minute head start over the person behind me. Maybe more if I make sure no one follows me to Jace's bar.

Slipping out through the back gate into the alley, I circle around to the main drag, poking my head out first to make sure I'm not being observed as I dart across the street into the bushes on one side of the park, then taking the most direct route to the bar without anyone else realizing where I'm headed. As I drop to my hands and knees, crawling through the shade beneath the prickly limbs, grateful I wore leggings and tennis shoes instead of my sundress, I swear I hear Beatrice's laugh. She has the best laugh—full and free and jam-packed with joy that lifts my heart every time I hear it.

But of course, I'm imagining things.

Wishing for things I need to stop wishing for.

Beatrice is an ocean away, and it will likely be a very, *very* long time until I see her again. If I ever see her again—which I might not, if Colin is cranky about the way I left or hires a better nanny who Beatrice loves so much she forgets about me entirely by the time school starts up next year.

The thought makes my "allergies" act up again, and by the time I emerge from the other end of the row of bushes, there are tears in my eyes. Scrambling to my feet, I swipe the backs of my hands across my cheeks, roll my shoulders back, and jog toward the bar.

I have to stop thinking about Beatrice and Colin. I have to stay focused on the task at hand. And once I win, I'll stay focused on cleaning up my house and getting resettled in Happy Cat. At least I won't have to worry about running into my evil, sheep-screwing ex-husband. Steve went to prison for setting fire to my factory, with my sister in it, and won't be bothering me —or any farm animals—anytime soon.

And I swear, that's the exact thought running through my head as I push through the door into The

Wild Hog to see my ex sitting at the bar, laughing with a woman in a fluffy white jacket and even fluffier blond hair eerily reminiscent of a sheep's spring fleece.

"Oh, hell, no," I shout before I can stop myself, thrusting a finger toward Steven's stupid fat head. "Get out! Get out right now!"

3

Colin

I GET MIXED UP TRYING TO FIND THE FIREHOUSE, BUT LUCK is on my side. I don't spy a single fire engine, but I do spot Savannah dashing into an establishment covered in brightly colored beer signs as I'm spinning in circles trying to orient myself in this town.

My heart leaps, and before my brain can engage, my feet are in motion. I have no idea what I'll say when I catch up with her, but I need to be at her side. The very sight of her fills me with bone-melting relief, joy, and a peace I took for granted while she was living in my house. I can't wait another moment to tell her how I feel.

I have to confess everything and beg her to give me a chance at her heart.

I swing through the door practically on her heels and then stutter to a stop as her shriek fills my ears.

There's a man in a cowboy hat seated at the bar beside a woman in a fluffy jacket that makes her resemble one of Bea's stuffed animals, and the bartender is vaulting across the counter to push between them.

"Van! You're home," the bartender says. "Hey. Come sit down. Over here. Way over here. You want a Savanny Sunshine? You loved it so much the last time you were in town, we named it after you and put it on the menu."

"Don't patronize me!" Van shouts.

The bartender lifts his arms in the air. "I'm not, I just—"

"*You're just serving the sheep-poker and his latest sheep!*"

Well.

This is suddenly awkward.

While Savannah and I have never talked openly about her ex-husband and his proclivities, I did a thorough background investigation on her before hiring her to be Beatrice's nanny three years ago, and I have far more knowledge of this situation than I'd like.

I also have unexpected rage and the urge to strangle a complete stranger.

"That man is supposed to be in prison," I announce.

Savannah spins, gasps, and goes sheet-white. "*Colin?*"

Those gorgeous bright eyes sweep over me, and I'm

unable to determine if that's joy, shock, or horror making her body sway uneasily.

Please be joy. Please, please be joy…

The bartender slips an arm around her, doing the very thing I ache to do myself, and I experience another surge of rage, but this one is mostly inspired by jealousy. White-hot, green-eyed monster-fueled jealousy.

Who the devil does he think he is? Laying hands on my Savannah?

"He's out on a technicality," the bartender says quietly, widening his eyes pointedly at me over Savannah's shoulder. "None of us are happy about it."

"You don't bloody well have to *serve* him though, do you?" I snap, widening my eyes back at him in return.

"According to anti-discrimination policies around here, yeah, I do. And who, exactly, are *you* to tell me how to run my bar?" he throws back.

"Yeah, ninnypants," the cowboy sheep-fucker says. "Who exactly are *you*?"

"He's my gorgeous English lover!" Savannah proclaims. "And he gives me *so many orgasms*. And he cares that I come first. And he goes down on me all the time. He goes down on me like it's his reason for living, and it's *so good* that I *go blind*. Seven times a night!"

The bartender shifts uncomfortably.

My shaft also shifts, though if we weren't in public, it would *not* be uncomfortable.

And my heart—my heart sees this for what it is. I'm not the man Savannah loves, but I *am* the man who can play her hero in this moment.

I clear my throat and utter a sentence I never dreamed I would be saying in public today.

"Quite right. I do rather enjoy a good pussy-licking."

Van's jaw drops.

The bartender shifts away from her even more, awkwardly rubbing his neck and looking to the bar as though it can save him from this infernally embarrassing conversation.

And the man in the cowboy hat—Savannah's ex-husband, Steve, the cheating bastard who tried to kill her sister and *got out of prison on a technicality*—sneers at me.

And I find that's the very last bloody straw.

I clear my throat again. "And I do mean her fanny. Not an actual cat. Unlike some people, I don't fornicate with animals."

"Ew, he licks her butt?" the wooly-jacketed woman whispers.

Americans. Honestly, I don't know how Savannah survived growing up here.

But whatever her origins, she found her way into my life, and the only thing that matters now is protecting her from this awful situation. "Savannah, love, would you like to join me for a cup of tea?"

"*No!*" She blinks, then cringes, looks back at her ex-husband and his sheep-woman, then steps closer to hiss in a softer voice, "We need to finish the treasure hunt. I have to sing."

"Fuck me," her ex mutters. "Can this day get any

worse? She sounds like a feral hyena being humped by a whale when she sings."

"That's it. Get the fuck out, Steve," the bartender orders.

"I'm waiting on my drink."

"You're harassing my customers."

"I have every right to—*urp*."

Well.

It seems the man's shirt collar has somehow ended up in my fist. However did that happen? "If you don't leave this premises at once," I growl into his started face, "I'll be happy to demonstrate how we handle sheep-fuckers where I come from."

I've honestly no clue how we handle sheep-fuckers in Britain. I practice law as a barrister, but that's not my specialty, nor an area of interest I've ever had any desire to research. But I do quite enjoy watching Steve's face pale to the shade of gray wool.

"N-no," he stammers, sweat breaking out on his upper lip.

His companion bounces off her stool onto her feet. "Come on, Steve. Let's go."

"No," he squeaks again, sounding even less sure of himself than before.

"If you don't come with me, I'm leaving by myself," she huffs. "And I'm taking this coat off and never putting it back on again, no matter how much you beg."

"Oh-okay." He glances her way and nods, though he's clearly a trite uncertain. "Okay. Let's go."

I shove him away, and she takes him—also by the collar—and drags him out of the bar.

And that leaves Savannah, me, and the nosy bartender.

"Savannah, love, could we—" I start.

She cuts me off with a wave of her hand. "Thank you, Colin, for the rescue, but you don't have to pretend in front of Jace. Now, I would very much like to know what you're doing here, and I'm sure we'll get around to that, but I'm a little preoccupied at the moment. And I have to sing—" She cuts herself off and looks at Jace. "I *do* have to sing for my next clue, don't I?"

He swipes a hand over his face as though it's a painful question. "Yes."

"Well, I'd like to get on with it before everyone else gets here. I'm winning right now."

"That actually depends on how you define winning." Jace cringes again and looks at the door, which is shutting behind Steve and his new woman.

She gasps. "*Steve* is winning the treasure hunt?"

"I didn't give him the clue, but Van, you know Steve. He grabbed one of the cards from the box behind the bar while I was swapping out a keg."

"The *cheater*." She shakes her hands out. "Turn on the music! I have to sing! I need my clue! I have to win this freaking competition!"

"Okay! Okay!" He backs away with his hands held up in surrender again. "What's your song?"

"My song? I don't know," she wails. "I hate singing in public!"

"Shall I sing for you?" I offer. She's bloody adorable when she's frustrated, and it happens so rarely that I would rather enjoy an opportunity to play hero for her. Again. If she'll let me. "Or we could…we can be a team." *Please, Savannah. Please understand I want to be on your team.*

Jace is fiddling with a computer next to the stage on the other side of the bar. "Pick a song, Van," he calls out. "If someone else comes in here yelling for me to cue up 'It's Raining Men' before you decide, I have to do it."

"'Wannabe,'" I blurt.

Savannah lifts her eyes to mine again. "Colin, no, you don't—"

"Put on the damned song. 'Wannabe.' Spice Girls. A man doesn't cross the pond in the middle of the night to—"

"'Respect,' Jace!" an older woman crows as she pushes through the door. "Put on some Aretha for me! I want that next clue!"

And that's how I end up on a karaoke stage in a small bar in the middle of Georgia, performing a Spice Girls song for Savannah in front of a group of women in matching electric pink tee shirts, to get her the next clue in her treasure hunt for love.

4

I can't breathe.

My heart has decided breathing is too difficult, and my lungs are too shocked to start a fight about it because Colin is *here*. Here. In Happy Cat.

And I know he's only here because he would do anything for Beatrice, and he had such a hard time finding a nanny for her before fate flung me into their lives. *And* he doesn't like change. He's not really here for *me,* not in that way.

But he sang so I didn't have to. And he told everyone he was my pussy-kissing boyfriend so that I didn't look like a loser in front of Steve, and he threatened to disembowel my ex-husband since the courts have apparently failed to provide justice.

But he would've done that for any lady in distress.

Beneath his gruff exterior, Colin is a total knight in shining armor. And a literal knight too. I found out from the neighbors that he was knighted as a teenager after he saved a bunch of puppies someone had thrown into a burlap sack and tossed in the river. Queen Elizabeth got word of his heroism and summoned him to London for an official knighting the very next weekend. So, he clearly has a history of being brave and protecting the innocent, and he's modest about it too.

I'm not special.

He isn't madly in love with me the way I'm madly in love with him.

He's just doing his knightly duties.

But he's tagging along as we race through Happy Cat to get to my house, where Cassie's kept my bicycle in good shape. And the next clue requires my bicycle, no question.

"*This* is your bicycle?" Colin asks.

I grip the purple dildo handlebars and refuse to be embarrassed. "Yep. Sex positivity is very important for women. You'll have to make sure Beatrice's next nanny can teach her that so that she'll never be ashamed of her body or let anyone else make her ashamed of it, either."

"Savannah—"

"So!" I nod toward the house next door. "You can borrow Ryan's bicycle if you want to come along with me. But it's okay if you don't. I'm over the shock of seeing Steve. I'll be okay on my own. I really will."

"Savannah—"

"But we can't waste any more time, and biking

around the lake is the fastest way to get to the Kennedy Family Day School."

At least, I hope the Kennedy Family Day School is where we're supposed to go. This clue wasn't as straightforward.

True love is like a hidden gem, sometimes you don't even know it's there. But once you find it, there's no mistaking the beauty, aroma, and music. For your next clue, find that hidden gem, and search the hearts within.

It could fit Maud and Gerald's shop, *Dough on the Square*, just as easily as it could fit the Kennedy Family Day School around the lake.

I bite my lip and look at Colin. "Or maybe we should split up. You could go to Dough on the Square and text me if you find the clue there, and I can head to the Day School."

"Savannah—"

"Oh, you're right. *Dammit*. Cheaters never win." I blow out a breath "Okay. To the Day School we go. This way. Follow me!"

"Savannah, could we please discuss—"

"Later, Colin." I leap on my bike and push the pedal to get going. "I can't risk Steve getting there first!"

Even knowing Steve is a cheater—and that if he cheats to win the magic love prize, it will do him zero good—doesn't offer much comfort.

Olivia's right.

Cheating darkens the world and the auras of everyone around the lying scumbags who do it.

We have to get to the Day School first. And it *has* to

be the Day School that the clue is referring to. Cassie introduced me to it when I came home for Olivia's wedding to Jace, and it fits the clue. The old building has been repurposed from its school roots to the best coffee and sandwich shop in the entire county, if not in all of Georgia, and somehow, it's a local gem that only a few people know about.

There's no way the clue could mean Maud and Gerald's donut shop on the square—everyone knows about that, and half the town has been buying their special treats there for decades.

Following my heart and the path behind my old house—right next door to where Cassie and Ryan are raising Logan—I head toward the school.

I hear what sounds like Colin riding along behind me, but I don't turn to look. If I turn to look, I might start believing that the magic of the treasure hunt is already working and that Colin's not here because he wants his nanny back for his daughter but because he wants me for himself. Because he loves me.

But even if he *does* love me, he probably wouldn't want me if he knew my baby maker is a big old diseased dud.

Colin is a great dad, and he's let it slip a few times that he wished he and his wife could have had more babies. And Beatrice is always pretending that she has younger sisters when she plays alone in her room. It breaks my heart, sometimes, hearing her boss and tease these imaginary siblings she might never have.

Colin and Beatrice both deserve a woman who can

help grow their family, not a chick with a pelvis that looks like the witch from Sleeping Beauty put a curse on her fallopian tubes.

"Savannah," he calls from behind me, making my stupid heart leap. But I can't help it. I'm glad he's following me, even if we're on a road to nowhere. "Could we please pause a moment? I have something very important to—*aaaahhhh!*"

I whip a glance over my shoulder and shout, *"George! Get off Colin's handlebars RIGHT NOW!"*

That damned raccoon. He must have been hiding in Ryan's bike basket. Now, he's going to cost me the treasure hunt, and I can't afford to wait another year to win.

For the past twenty years, every person who's won the treasure hunt has found their true love within just a few months. The first year, everyone laughed at the funny coincidence, the second year, eyebrows were raised, and by the third year, it had become downright eerie. But in a good way. In Happy Cat, people aren't afraid of a little spooky stuff, as long as the spooky ends in two lonely hearts finding happiness.

No one has questioned it since, which is why our local singles aren't the only ones zipping around town like love-thirsty beavers today. People come from all around Georgia to win big in the treasure hunt of love.

This year is *my year*. I know the universe wants to give me that gift—I can feel it in my love-hungry bones. I'm ready to give my heart away in a way I've never been before. Even with Steve, back when he was a better human and marrying him seemed like a fun idea, if not my romantic dream, I always held back a part of myself. I just wasn't ready to open up to another person that way, not even the man I loved.

But now I know what it's like to truly be alone—alone in a foreign country, alone in a city where everyone seems cooler and more put together than I am, and alone in my bed every night with no one to snuggle when I'm sad, let alone anything more. That loneliness has taught me many things, including that I *can* stand on my own two feet, even when it's hard. But it's also taught me that holding the people you love at arm's length is stupid.

I've promised myself that if I'm ever lucky enough to find that perfect-for-me man, I won't hold back. I'll dive into the love ocean and swim hard, no matter how rough the waves might get.

But right now, my sister's pet raccoon is sabotaging my efforts and making my unexpected escort veer off the path and into the woods. "Brake, Colin!" I call as I switch course to circle back to rescue him. "*Brake!* George can handle himself!"

Colin's bumping and swerving on the bike as he hits every exposed tree root and fallen branch in his way, heading toward the lake just beyond the trees, making me wonder where he learned to ride a bike.

Wait a second. Have I ever seen him on a bike?

I don't think I have.

And now George is chittering and climbing onto Colin's head as he tries to steer them both to safety, I'm off-roading on my bike that was *not* built for this terrain, and honestly, I'm out of practice with biking too.

"Colin, *brake!*" I yell one last time.

But it's too late. He hits a massive rock, and the bike slides sharply to the right. George goes flying off into the woods as Colin crashes and burns in a fairly spectacular fashion.

Pulse racing, I ditch my bike and run the rest of the way to his side. "*Colin!*"

"What in the *bloody hell* is wrong with that *ridiculous* animal?"

I drop to my knees beside him as he sits up, swiping at the fallen live oak leaves coating his clothing and crumbled in his hair. He's adorably mussed and dirty. It reminds me of the first time Beatrice and I came home from playing in the park, not long after I started as her nanny, both of us covered in sweat and dirt.

He'd looked the two of us over, sighed heavily, and walked away shaking his head, as if getting messy in the out of doors was akin to getting caught picking your nose in church.

Unlike the *last* time Beatrice and I came home from the park, when we'd been chased by geese and accidentally fallen into the Serpentine, getting soaked to the skin.

I'd known Colin had an important after-hours call in his study that day, and I'd told Beatrice we needed to be quiet as we came inside. But he must have seen us sloshing our way up the sidewalk outside from his office because he met us at the door with towels, announced he was putting on the kettle to fix us a cuppa to warm us up, and hadn't said a word about his call being interrupted or the mess we left in the foyer.

If anything, he just seemed happy that we were safe and on our way to being dry and that Beatrice had a new adventure to add to her ever-growing list. He even praised her bravery and dubbed her Beatrice, the Brave, slayer of geese and defender of innocent American nannies.

My love for him grew even more that day.

That a man as rigid and exacting as Colin could learn to live with the extra messes that I brought into his life in the name of his little girl's happiness proved he wasn't cold or heartless.

When we first met, he was a young widower constantly handling *one more thing* and struggling in ways that he tried and often failed to hide, but now—

Now, he's so much more.

To me, at least.

"Are you hurt?" I ask, smoothing his hair from his forehead. I frown as I see how pale he is. "You don't look good."

"I'm fine," he says, the muscle in his jaw going tight.

"You don't look fine. Is it your head? Does it hurt? What about your ankles, your knees?"

"Savannah, please."

"What about your hips? Elbows? Are you bruised? Does anything feel broken?" My hands are all over him by this point—gently probing and testing. My heart is pounding again. I've never touched him like this, never dared take the liberty, but I need to know he's in one piece.

I need to know he's not hurt.

Even if he'll never be mine, I always want him to be safe and happy and healthy. I just love him so much. It hits me again, bringing tears to my eyes as he catches my hands in his.

I gasp softly at the touch, then swallow hard as his eyes meet mine.

"I'm fine," he says quietly, his gaze holding me captive. "Physically, anyway. Emotionally, however, I fear I'm a bit of a wreck."

5

Colin

THIS IS IT. THE PERFECT MOMENT.

She's here. I'm here. We're alone in a lovely patch of forest with a light breeze blowing her hair around her face and her eyes telling me she's ready to hear everything I've been dying to tell her. She cares for me. Or at least cares whether or not I've split my head open falling off the first bicycle I've ridden in twenty years.

I need to tell her how I feel.

Now.

With all that's already gone wrong in the short time since I found her, it's clear that this might be the only chance I'll get. I pull in a breath, sweep my tongue across my lips, and…choke.

My mouth opens and closes with no words coming

out and nothing but a sharp, panicked humming sound vibrating through my head as though a hummingbird from Bea's favorite American picture book has taken up residence inside my skull. Suddenly fears I haven't even considered before begin crawling out of my brain like zombies bursting from the grave, ready to put an end to this romance before it begins.

What if Savannah has no use for a boyfriend who's also a single dad? I know she loves Beatrice with all her heart, but that doesn't mean she's ready to step up and be her mother.

A nanny is quite different from a mother. A nanny is paid to care for a child, gets time off, and isn't obligated to participate in family movie nights or board games after hours. A nanny can leave the more severe reprimands to the parent, and a nanny is free to participate in the fun and frolic of child-rearing, rather than the intimidating business of ensuring a small human grows up to be a sane, happy, helpful grown human.

Did Savannah leave because the reality of another eight years of raising someone else's child was too much?

She *did* say she needed to focus on her own life.

And she deserves her own family for all of those momentous occasions that we, as humans, celebrate with the ones we love.

"Colin, are you—" Her words end in a startling yipping sound as the damned raccoon suddenly leaps over my shoulder to plop down in the leaves between us. "Oh my God, George. You scared the crap out of me. And you nearly killed Colin."

"I'm fine," I say, arching a brow as the little beastie rolls over on his back and grins up at me, like he's pulled off an incredible prank. "How intelligent are these animals?"

"Very. Huge brains, fast learners, and better problem solvers than your average three-year-old. And after hearing all the trouble Logan gets up to when Cassie's back is turned, I have a new level of respect for that metric. Logan isn't even two yet."

George scratches his large belly and then stretches his arms over his head and glances at Savannah, as if waiting for a high five. She giggles and obliges. "Fine, you wretched little thing. But no more popping out of baskets. It's a good thing you've played hero so often around here. But you're still going to hurt someone someday." She sighs and glances over her shoulder. "Or just ruin their chances of treasure hunt domination."

"You really want to win this thing, don't you? It isn't just about beating your ex."

"That would be the whipped cream on the banana split, but no, it's not about him." She rubs George's belly as she adds in a softer voice, "It's about me. About proving that I'm ready and that the universe sees that."

I don't ask *ready for what?*

It's a treasure hunt for love, after all.

While I seriously doubt a bunch of silly clues are going to help her find it, if this is her dream, then I'll do whatever it takes to help that dream come true. Even if it means breaking my own heart in the process.

After all, if *I* were the focus of her affection, she wouldn't have left the way she did. She's here for a fresh start and to find a partner who isn't me. She might even already have one in mind. She might be planning to win first place and head right back to the bar and that touchy-feely bartender who was far too good-looking for his own good.

Or even back to England.

Bollocks.

She could have a boyfriend *in England,* and I wouldn't know.

The thought of her in love with anyone else makes my blood hotter, but I push aside the temptation to plot yet another man's demise and rise to my feet. "Then let's get going," I say, reaching a hand down to Van.

She shakes her head. "No, it's too late. We've lost too much time, and I'm not even sure I was headed the right way."

"No doubting yourself after you've come this far," I say. "You're unstoppable when it comes to solving puzzles, and you always predict the plot twist five minutes after the movie's started. It's diabolical."

Her lips quirk. "That's different—once you work in television for a while, you just know what a story needs —but thank you. I like being called diabolical. It feels fancy. And smart."

"You are fancy and smart *and* diabolical and made of

tougher stuff than this. We don't get to the finish line and lie down for a nap, Savannah. That's when we push even harder. That's when we give it our all."

She laughs. "You sound like an exercise video."

"Thank you," I say, curling two fingers. "Come on, up you go. Back on that bike. Lead the way, and I'll follow."

"You will?" Her plaintive, hopeful voice makes me think she's talking about more than this bike ride or the treasure hunt.

My heart lifts as a second, perfect moment presents itself. All I have to do is open my mouth and tell her that yes, I will follow her anywhere. That I'll follow her to the moon and back if that's what it takes to win her heart. Hell, that I'll give up my life in London, my job, my house, everything I've worked for, and move half a world away to a town named after sexually satisfied female genitalia if that's what it takes.

I *need* to tell her.

I need to take this risk, despite all the reasons I'm positive she'll reject me. One cannot hear *yes* if one doesn't ask the question, and if there's anything I've learned in three years of having Savannah in my house, teaching Bea—and me—the value of embracing joy, of trying new things, and of sheer belief, it's that leaps of faith are worth taking.

The biggest risks are necessary if a man is to achieve the greatest rewards.

And I'm about to do it. The words are right there, an

eloquent confession even my jaded heart thinks might have a chance of winning the girl.

But before I can speak, adolescent male voices echo through the woods, coming from the same direction we did a few moments ago.

"Come on, hurry up," one shouts. "We're the first ones on the trail!"

"Okay, but don't go too fast," the other shouts back. "That raccoon lives somewhere out here. That thing's freaky as hell. My mom says it's probably packed with diseases and that's why it acts weird."

"Did you hear that, George?" I ask, glancing down at the raccoon who does, amazingly, look rather cheesed off. It's as if it actually understands what the boy said and isn't happy about it. "Think you can slow them down for us?"

Van pulls in a breath, like she needs to protest, and I hurry on with my final orders to the raccoon. "No cheating, just a little…creative interference."

George lets out a positively gleeful string of chatter and bounds off in the direction of the voices. I reach my hand down to Savannah again. "Come, my lady. Get up and go after your dreams. I'll be right behind you."

"Beside me." She takes my hand and lets me draw her to her feet. "You should stay beside me. So I can keep an eye on you, in case you get into trouble again."

I'm already in trouble. Too much trouble.

I'm in love with a woman who's clearly decided she wants something different from life than what I have to offer, and it fucking sucks.

But I don't say any of that. I simply nod, pick up my bike, and climb back to the trail beside her, doing my best to memorize the slope of her nose and the way the sun catches her hair, wanting to remember every second of this day, the last one I might ever have with the woman I love.

6

Savannah

THANKS TO OUR BIKES, WE'RE THE FIRST ONES TO THE Kennedy Family Day School, but now I'm nervous that Steve and his lady friend have been here and are already on to the next clue. We were in the woods for *a while*.

Or maybe it just seemed like a long time because I kept having mini-heart attacks, hoping Colin was going to say what I thought he was going to say—that he adores me the way I adore him and wants to spend the rest of his life making more beautiful memories together.

But no. No confession was forthcoming. Just some sweet encouragement from my former boss who clearly believes in me and wants my dreams to come true. He just doesn't want to play a major part in them.

Sob!

I *will* cry about all that later. I know I will. But now isn't the time for tears. I can't afford to waste any more time, not if there's even a cherry snow cone's chance in hell that I'm the first hunter to arrive at the cute café.

Colin and I set our bikes beside the porch and race inside the sandwich shop and general store that was once an abandoned schoolhouse. I know the teenage boys aren't far behind—we heard them shout about ten minutes ago when George did whatever it was George decided to do—but we're definitely still in the lead.

Also, teenage boys have *plenty* of time to find their true love.

Their parents will be grateful that George is slowing them down.

"Have we gone back in time?" Colin asks as we push through the doors and into the coffee-scented air. "Is this what America was like in the pioneer days?"

"It's living history," I tell him.

"Charming. Do they serve tea as well?"

"*Savannah?*"

Colin and I both turn at the sound of a masculine voice. "Blake?" My jaw drops. "You O'Dell brothers are everywhere today. What are you doing here?" I ask as Ryan and Jace's other brother sets aside two mugs of coffee and envelops me in a hug.

I miss hugs from family, and since Blake is Cassie's brother-in-law, he's close enough for me to call him family too. And his hug feels good—safe and sane and a silent promise that everything is going to be all right.

Coming home was good for me.

If only Colin weren't still beside me, making me wish *he* would hug me too.

And then kiss me.

And touch me everywhere I've fantasized about for so long.

When he went along with my lie that he loved to go down on me for hours… Well, that was total fiction, but the thought of it is dizzying. I can't think about it for more than a second or two or I'll go absolutely mad.

"I'm here helping out with the event," Blake says.

I pull back, thrilled at this stroke of luck. It's clearly one more sign that I'm supposed to win. "How perfect! I'm on a mission to find a clue. Got any hints you can share?"

He laughs beneath his breath. "Van, you know you're my favorite former child star ever, but I can't just tell you."

I make puppy dog eyes. I don't know why Blake's helping *here*—he has a winery, and his wife runs a small rescue farm—but he clearly knows something, and I'd bet this is a sign that I can mark both the winery and Hope's farm off the list of potential next places for hidden clues. "I know. That's why I asked for a hint. Just a teeny tiny hint. *Please?*"

"Why is that llama wearing a string of illuminated hearts?" Colin asks.

Blake's eye twitches, my mental wheels turn, and everything clicks. I spin and grab Colin by the hand. I'd bet Beatrice's favorite doll that Colin's just spotted an alpaca, not a llama. Electricity shoots up my arm from the spot where our palms connect, and Colin's warm eyes fix even more firmly on mine, as though he, too, has felt the jolt.

Not just felt it but *welcomed* it.

But—*no*.

That's not in the cards for the two of us.

For the millionth time, Savannah, move on.

I snatch my hand back. "Wh-where did you see it?" I ask.

Colin glances down at my waist, where I'm now twisting my hands together, then nods out the window overlooking the grassy picnic area behind the school. "Out there."

Blake's wife, Hope, is outside breastfeeding her baby at one of the picnic tables while two of her alpacas stand guard.

I glance back at Blake, who gives me a secret smile. "Yeah, I can't hand out hints, Van, but I'm *positive* Hope would love to see you. And if you haven't met Baxter yet, my son would be delighted to see you too."

I go up on the tippy-top of my tiptoes to throw my arms around him again and peck his cheek. "Thank you! I'll tell Hope you win the prize for best brother-in-law ever, okay? C'mon, Colin! The next clue is out here!"

I almost grab his hand again, but I catch myself just in time.

He touches his fingertips to the small of my back. "After you."

A delicious shiver tickles up my spine and wraps out around my ribs, and my voice comes out breathy as I say, "Thank you."

"You're welcome," he replies, the tenderness in his voice making me ache all over again.

Why can't he be my treasure at the end of this hunt? Why? Could I arrange for the O'Dell brothers to kidnap him, wrap him in the traditional shiny silver wrapping paper, and hide him at the end of the hunt? I mean, a medal with a grinning cat on it imbued with magical powers is great and all, but who needs a medal when you have a drop-dead gorgeous man with a huge heart who makes you feel magical just for waking up in the morning?

The way he's smiled at me when I stepped into the breakfast room every day for the past few months made me feel special. Wanted. But now he seems eager to help me win a contest all but guaranteed to throw me into another man's arms.

Ugh. Why are feelings this confusing?

Shaking off the moment, I turn and wave to Blake, who's watching both Colin and me rather curiously. "Thanks so much! Let's catch up later!" I call as we head out the back door.

Hope greets me with a wide grin that transforms into raised-brow curiosity as Colin follows me across the bright spring grass, her gaze shifting back and forth between us. "Hey, Savannah. Cassie just sent a group text letting everyone know that you're here and partici-pating in the treasure hunt. How fun is this? You came home at a great time. I can't wait to catch up on all your news and hear all of your stories. There's no way Blake and I can leave the country for any adventures of our own, what with the farm and the winery, so I need to live vicariously through you."

"Yes, yes, you adorable human with your adorable baby," I say, ignoring the flash of pain that shoots through my chest at the sight of her sweet, sleepy boy nodding off on her breast. I'm happy for her and Blake, but the news that I'll never know what it's like to nurse a sweet little one is still too fresh. My feelings about almost everything are complicated right now. "But first, give me the goods. I'm ready for the next clue."

Her lips twitch. "No guesses first?"

"Something to do with that llama, I'd imagine," Colin suggests.

"*Alpaca*," Hope corrects. "But I'll forgive you for the mistake, because your accent is utterly delicious."

"Ah, thank you." He shifts, his face doing that endearing thing that it does when he walks in on Beatrice and me having a conversation about puberty or boys.

"Aw, and that blush is charming." Hope grins as she shifts her attention back to me and subtly wiggles her brows, silently asking the question I've asked myself a dozen times today alone.

Is there something going on between Colin and me?

The answer is no. Probably. Most likely. Unless I'm confused.

I'm definitely the last part so I shrug and roll my

eyes, hopefully telegraphing, "*I have no idea, we'll dish later,*" and point to the alpaca wearing the heart necklace. "Okay, the clue did say something about hearts." I pull it from my pocket and read it aloud. "Beauty, hearts, aroma… Search the hearts within…" I look up, delight rushing through my chest. "Oh my gosh, do we get to hug your alpacas?"

"Well, that's a start." Hope's smile has turned downright devious.

"For heaven's sakes, must we woo the thing?" Colin asks.

It's so very *Colin* in that grumpy yet resigned way that my heart flutters once again.

She giggles. "As much fun as that would be to watch, no. Just a hug and a peck on the cheek. Chewpaca has been working very hard on his new trick, but he knows he has to get a hug *and* a kiss first."

The alpaca wanders closer at the sound of his name, lips flapping like one of my former dates who was entirely too excited at the idea of the post-date kiss, though on Chewpaca, the sweet thing, it's darling. Colin frowns hard—very hard—but doesn't move away.

"Get in there, you two." Hope waves her free hand, gesturing us closer to the animal, as the baby squirms in his sleep. "Don't be shy. Or nervous. Chewpaca is the sweetest lover in all the land. I wouldn't have him be a part of an event if I didn't know he would behave himself."

"Hope runs a rescue farm and is amazing with all

animals," I tell Colin, stepping around to the large, oh-so-soft creature's other side. "So, on the count of three? We hug and peck at the same time?"

"I'd do the count of one," Hope says. "You're the first team here, but I'm betting the others aren't far behind, and the next stop is pretty far away." She curses softly, casts a glance at the baby like she doesn't want him hearing bad words, and brings a hand to cover her mouth. "Shoot, I shouldn't have told you that. Pretend I didn't."

"Pretend what? I heard nothing." I turn back to Colin with a firm nod, my heart soaring at the knowledge that Steve hasn't beaten us here. But has he cheated in another way?

No. I won't worry about that either. I'll simply embrace this moment and know that I'm doing this race *right.* I add a smile and nod to Colin. "Ready? And…one."

Our arms wrap around Chewpaca's neck, tangling together in a way that's so nice I'm distracted for a moment. By the time I remember it's time to go in for the kiss and tilt my head back to aim my mouth at the alpaca's cheek, the handsome boy is gone, replaced by an even handsomer one. It's Colin, with his eyes closed, aiming his lips toward the same empty air as mine.

Before I can reverse direction, our mouths collide.

It's not romantic at all—at least not at first—but after the initial startle of surprise on his part and muttered apologies on my part, I find every inch of my skin humming with a case of the tingles unlike anything I've experienced since Colin hefted me off that countertop. Because he doesn't pull away. He steps into the space Chewpaca has left behind, wraps an arm around my waist, pulls me tight against him, and deepens the kiss.

For a moment, I'm keenly aware that we have an audience—Hope is making a happy cooing sound, or maybe that's Chewpaca, I'm not sure—but soon awareness of everything but Colin's fantastic lips vanishes completely. His tongue slips past my lips with a controlled confidence as I melt against his strong chest, wishing this moment never had to end.

But it does end, with an alpaca snout shoved in between our faces and a happy purring sound that makes me laugh.

I press my hands to my hot cheeks as we pull apart.

Hope laughs, sounding half-apologetic, half gleeful. "Sorry! He just wants you to open one of his hearts and take the clue out. It's what he was trained to do. Otherwise, he'd never interrupt such nice kissing."

My devious but possibly perfect friend's eyes glitter as Colin reaches for one of the hearts.

I do my best to stop blushing.

"That was very nice kissing, by the way," she says innocently. "You two should do more of it. Though probably somewhere else. Where you won't be interrupted by alpacas or the smell of a rotten baby butt. Baxter always lets loose with something nasty after his afternoon feeding."

As if on cue, the baby gives forth an adorable grunt and a much less adorable juicy fart.

"Oh my God," I mutter as the smell starts to drift my way on the breeze. "The poor thing. That sounded painful."

"He'll be quite all right," Colin says as he scans the clue. "Beatrice was the same way as an infant. It's the one thing I don't miss about those baby years."

My soaring heart nosedives back toward the ground as his words remind me of my unhappy secret. Plus, he hasn't made eye contact with me since we broke the kiss. What does that mean?

Ugh. How do people survive falling in love? This up-and-down, emotional roller coaster is enough to make me want to run away *again,* just like I did three years ago when I found Steve cheating on me. And just like I did *yesterday* when I realized I couldn't keep pretending that Colin and Beatrice were my family when Colin doesn't love me the way I love him.

But—is he not making eye contact because he's embarrassed?

Or is it because he's afraid *I'm* embarrassed?

What if it did mean something to him? What if he *is* here for me, and not because he doesn't want to find Beatrice a new nanny, but because he wants *me?*

And if that kiss meant as much to Colin as it did to me, then I need to tell him *everything,* and everything could break his heart as much as it's breaking mine, and again, *why do people have to fall in love?*

When he hands me the clue and I instantly realize we're bound for the cemetery clear on the other side of

Happy Cat, I'm relieved. We'll have plenty of time to talk while we bike over.

And we should talk, even though I don't want to.

I don't want to know if he doesn't love me.

And if he does love me half as much as I've grown to love him, I don't want to have to tell him that I can't make all his dreams come true and that he might be better off finding someone else.

The thought makes my heart ache as we bid Hope goodbye and hurry back to fetch our bikes just as the two teen boys emerge from the woods covered in… feathers? How George managed that—and whether his nemesis, Nutquacker, the savage goose from heck, might be involved—is anyone's guess.

The world will probably never know exactly what went down in those woods, but I know I'm grateful to George. There's still a good chance I'll need that treasure hunt medal and the love magic that goes along with it, a fact Colin proves by scowling at me as we start off down the road, bound for a place where *love never dies.*

7

Colin

SHE KISSED ME.

I kissed her.

And the kiss was flat out fucking brilliant.

And then she decided to rush off to the next clue on this godforsaken hunt as if she wasn't affected at all by the chemistry that exploded between us. I'm sure that at some point in my life I've been more irritated than I am right now, but I can't remember when.

I want to jump off this bike, lift it over my head, and hurl it into the woods beside the road with a caveman's roar. Then I want to rip Savannah off her bike, toss her over my shoulder, and carry her to my cursed manor in the woods, where I will hold her prisoner until she comes to her senses and falls in love with me...proving

I've watched *Beauty and the Beast* with Beatrice far too many times.

But the beast *did* get the girl in the end.

And I'm feeling quite beastly in this moment.

Maybe a little kidnapping wouldn't be out of order. If I'm to fall apart and become a madman, then I might as well do it right.

"You're losing your mind," I mutter beneath my breath. "Pull it together, man."

"What's that?" Savannah asks, sounding a little breathless from our hard push down this idyllic country lane.

"Nothing," I snap back. I should regret my tone, but I'm at my wit's end with this hunt and wanting to tell her how I feel and being terrified that she won't return my affections. I don't know how to be the rational, in-control man that I generally pride myself on being.

She huffs. "Right. I, um… I think we should talk."

"Why should we talk? Why stop this insanity now? By all means, let's keep racing toward the conclusion of this farce of a race so you can find true love. Heaven forfend I keep you from the completion of your course."

"I'm not sure what 'forfend' means because I was a child star and educated poorly on a television set, but I can read your tone," she says, huffing harder as we start up a small hill. "And that tone isn't a sunny, happy tone, Colin."

"Well, I'm not feeling very sunny, Savannah." I'm practically shouting now. The damned American-ness of this place is rubbing off on me already. "I'm frustrated and confused and unsure what you experienced back there. I, for one, experienced one of the best kisses of my life."

She sucks in a sharp breath, and her front wheel wobbles a little before she regains control of her bike. "Me too. The very best ever, but there are things you don't know about me, Colin. Things that you aren't going to like."

Bloody hell. *Why* must women always be so confounding? How on earth could there be a single thing about Savannah Sunderwell that *any* man could object to? "What sort of things? I know you aren't a fugitive from justice. I had your background checked before I offered you the position as Bea's nanny. And I don't see that you'd have had time to commit international espionage or start a drug cartel on your one day off a week since then."

She glares at me over her shoulder. "I'm very good at causing trouble for myself and absolutely could become a spy in my spare time if I wanted to."

I snort.

"I could," she insists. "I'm a very good actress. But no, I'm not involved in espionage. And I hate drugs. At least bad drugs. Wine and pot are pretty great in moderation, especially when you're stressed. Like now, for example. Maybe we should swing into Jace's bar after we win the hunt and grab a beer or something before we talk. Doesn't a beer sound like it would make everything better?"

"No, it does not. And I don't like that man. He's handsy."

She looks back at me again, but this time, her expression is different, as is her tone. She's *grinning*, the minx. "He's married, quite happily so, to my very best friend. But it's cute that you were jealous. You were jealous, correct? I'm reading that super grumpy growl that just came out of your mouth correctly?"

I answer her with a glare that makes her laugh, though her glee fades as she speaks. "You *were* jealous. I probably shouldn't be happy about that. But I am. But I also know we need to talk. *Really* talk. Neither one of us has done a very good job of communicating lately, Colin. Or possibly ever."

My scowl softens as I admit, "You're right. And I'm not mad at you. I…adore you."

"I adore you too," she says, her voice soft and a little sad. "I adore you so much that I can't let this go any further until you know the truth."

I'm about to demand, yet again, that she tell me this forbidding truth—I can't imagine there's anything that could dissuade me from doing whatever it takes to make her mine—when an errant hell-beast double the size of a Sunday roast bursts out of the underbrush beside the lane, squawking and flapping its mutant wings right in front of Savannah.

She shrieks and swerves, and for the second time today, I do the same, sending my bicycle skidding and myself tumbling into the dirt.

"Nutquacker!" Savannah cries.

The blasted beast circles me, honking and flapping while my nanny, Bea's favorite person, the woman I've fallen desperately in love with, once again comes to my rescue, chasing the animal—the bird?—until it's honking at the side of the road.

"We *do not* chase people off of bicycles." Savannah shakes a finger at the creature as I pick myself up off the dusty lane and survey the situation. The animal looks rather like a half-plucked goose. "You know what happens when you terrorize the people who feed you. And what have you done with your feathers? Were you fighting with George again? Do I need to tell Hope what you've been up to?"

"What the *devil* are you doing?" If I'm the beast, Savannah is Snow White, communicating with the woodland creatures.

Have I hit my head?

Did I actually land in America several hours ago, or am I having the world's most awful dream?

"Nutquacker sometimes forgets his place, and he's ridiculous around strangers." She shifts between me and the goose, playing the hero once again. "Are you okay? I should've seen Nutquacker coming. Or heard him. He's hardly quiet. But I was—well, I was distracted."

Her gaze drops as the goose quiets itself. "Can we please finish the treasure hunt, and then actually sit down and talk? I know nothing's going exactly right, but I'm having a lovely time with you. And I can't explain it—not fully—but I *need* to win this. My friend Olivia is always telling me to follow the signs, and the signs say that I *have* to do this. Those boys won't be far behind us, even if Hope stalls them, and…"

I clear my throat and reach to adjust my tie, only to remember I'm not currently wearing a tie. My throat is tight for other reasons, ones only Savannah can resolve.

But I can wait to talk. Of course, I can. I can do whatever it takes to make her happy. "Let's finish this, then," I say, collecting my bike from the ground nearby.

Her smile returns. "Great. Thank you so much. And thank you, Nutquacker, for getting us back on track. Now, you can slow down the other hunters too, but do *not* hurt anyone. Understand?"

The goose gives her a menacing glare, then shakes its head and snort-honks.

"I mean it, Nutquacker."

The damned bird flops to the ground and pouts like a child.

"Good boy," Savannah says. "Colin, let's go. The cemetery isn't big, but there will be so many places to hide the next clue that we shouldn't waste any time."

I fear I've already wasted too much time with this woman. But if she's willing to let me accompany her on this quest, and is committed to talking afterwards, then this is time well-spent.

All time with Savannah is well-spent.

Especially since she clearly intends on presenting me with a very large *but* when we're finally able to discuss our situation and why mutual adoration might not be enough to ensure I leave Happy Cat with my family intact.

She's a part of my family now, one I can't bear to lose.

8

Savannah

WHEN I WAS AN ACTOR, I WAS ALWAYS ABLE TO TAP INTO my emotions and funnel them into my work. It gave me a safe place for all those big feelings to come out and play.

There was a script, after all, and we had to stick to it, not to mention a director and a showrunner and tons of other people tasked with making sure we stayed safe on set. My emotions couldn't hurt me back then. They were my tools, my talent, my superpower, what set me apart from other kids and made me a star.

When the show ended and my family returned to Happy Cat full time, those big feelings naturally found other outlets. I fell in and out of love with several local boys, launched a business I was passionate about, and eventually found Steve.

And then he broke my heart, and I realized just how dangerous real-life feelings could be. Real-life feelings weren't controlled or scripted. They were painful, unpredictable, and they made me hurt so much that all I wanted to do was escape. I *needed* that escape so badly that I abandoned my biggest pet project, Sunshine Sex Toys, and left it to Cassie for her to pick up the pieces.

But then I found Beatrice and Colin, and those feelings slowly started working their way to the surface again. I threw myself into loving Bea—I couldn't help myself, she's such a sweet, special kid. I learned what she, as a child, needed from me, how to give her that safe space to feel but also how to work through hard feelings without running away. I was rewarded by watching her grow in confidence, self-love, and happiness, and sometime in the middle of it all, I realized that *I* deserve happiness too.

And that it's okay for me to feel big things. And that I'm strong and brave enough to handle them, even when it's hard.

But right now, I'm afraid of all the big things I feel for Colin. *Especially* now, as we prop our bikes against the wooden fence surrounding the cemetery.

"Quite lovely for a graveyard," he says quietly.

"I used to be spooked by all the headstones," I confess, my voice hushed too, "but then Olivia helped me to see that these are places of peace. Plus, the clue was right. These people might be resting, but look how many are resting with their soulmates. *Love never dies.*"

"It's a lovely sentiment."

"Do you think it's true?"

He takes my hand, and the world stands still. "I do," he says, so quiet, so grave, so very *Colin*, so very perfect. "Love never dies. It's not stopped by time, or distance, or by any natural force of man. It lives and breathes, even if it scares us, even when we're afraid to put words to just how much we love someone."

My breath catches. "Have you ever known that kind of love?"

"I have." His free fingers brush my cheek. "I do. Today. Now. Here."

I can't lie to myself or blame my allergies this time when my eyes get hot and my throat clogs. "*Colin.*"

"My sweet Savannah, why do you think I flew halfway across the world at a moment's notice to find you?"

"Because you didn't want to bother finding another nanny?"

He shakes his head, somber and serious. "I fear I've fallen into the trap of being one more man not to realize what he had until she was gone."

"No, Colin," I say, fanning my eyes as I will the tears to dry up fast. "We can't do this now. We have to wait."

"I don't want to wait, not one more bloody minute. You've snuck into my heart, Savannah Sunderwell, and into my soul. I don't know who I am without you anymore, and I don't want to find out." He pulls in a bracing breath and tightens his grip on my hand. "I love you, Savannah. You're my joy. My light. And I—"

"Colin, I can't have children." I don't mean to blurt

it out that way, but I can't stop myself. I can't let him say one more word before he knows. He has to know. He has to have all the information and let it change his mind if that's what's right for him. Even if the thought of him changing his mind feels like it might kill me.

I stare at the green grass poking through the earth amidst the gravestones, going on about its grassy business as if the only thing that actually matters is that the sun comes up every morning after regular rain.

"If we were together," I continue. "I couldn't help you grow your family the way I know you want to."

"Savannah—"

"I'm broken," I whisper. "And there's nothing the doctors can do to fix it. I already had all the scans and tests and everything."

"Sweetheart. My darling girl." He takes my chin and lifts my face, forcing me to look at him. "You aren't broken. You are so far from broken, and if you think something like that might change my feelings for you, I'm afraid I haven't let you get to know me at all. I've flown across an ocean to tell you that I love you, Savannah. I forgot to pack socks. I nearly left my wallet on the airplane. I don't need you to bear my children. All I need, all I want, is you. Just you, the most wonderful, kind, frustrating, funny, caring, best woman I've ever known."

I press my lips together, my throat working as his words take root in my heart, filling me with the same peace, the same sense of rightness, the same joy I feel when I watch my sister laughing with her husband and toddler. When I chase kites through the park with Bea on a sunny day. When I have long talks with Olivia about trusting in the universe and knowing that goodness is out there and everything I really need is right here inside me.

But this peace and joy are bigger.

They're deeper.

They're *love*.

"You really love me?" I whisper. "Even with all my faults?"

"You wouldn't be you without them. And being unable to bear children is *not* a fault." He leans in as though he wants to kiss me but hesitates. "What about you? I know I can be a lot. And not always in a good way. I can be a grumpy know-it-all. And bossy. And controlling when it comes to sugar around the house."

"You can," I agree, a sound that's half laugh and half sob bursting from my lips. "But you're also kind and generous and devoted to your daughter. And I have so much fun with you, whether we're watching a movie or taking a walk through the park or chasing Beatrice into the waves."

"I'd like to take you to Spain again," he murmurs. "Just the two of us this time. Assuming…"

That's when I realize that I haven't said the words back.

They're clogged in my throat. I know they're right, but I'm still scared. I've never put my heart on the line like this before, not even with Steve. This is the kind of love I've always wanted, but it's also the biggest risk

I've ever taken. Happily ever after with Colin would be a beautiful dream come true. Trying-and-failing with Colin, however...

Well, I'm pretty sure that would break me in ways far more profound than anything I've experienced before.

Don't be scared, Savannah, I can hear Olivia whispering. *Don't be scared. Life is a journey, and you have all the tools to get you where you want to go. Let yourself take this turn and see where it leads.*

And so I push up on my tiptoes again, this time not to hug a friend, but to kiss the man that I love. "I love you," I whisper, inches from his lips, my heart flipping at the relieved sound that escapes him. "And now I'm going to kiss you like I mean it. Because I do."

He presses a finger to my lips, stopping me before I can seal the deal, and pulls back to smile down at me, his eyes shining just like mine probably are. "Not yet. First, we have a treasure hunt to win."

I shake my head slightly, loving the feel of his finger rough against my lips. "No, we don't. I already won. I'm leaving Georgia with a sexy new boyfriend who thinks I'm the best woman he's ever met. What more could a woman ask for?"

"I don't know," he says, brushing his fingertip back and forth over my bottom lip, sending tingles racing across my skin. "Perhaps staying in her hometown with her sexy new boyfriend who's willing to move to America in the name of keeping his sexy new girlfriend close to her friends and family who he knows she's missed desperately?"

My jaw drops, but before I can ask if he's serious, he continues, "And beating that sheep-fucking wanker might be nice. I, for one, would like to see his face when we win. And I'd like our first time together to be someplace a bit less morbid."

I blink. It takes a moment to realize what he means, but when I do, my heart pounds even faster. "Are you saying…?"

"I'm saying that if I start kissing you, I won't stop until your clothes are on the ground and my mouth is between your legs," he rumbles in the sexiest bedroom voice I've ever heard. "Someone mentioned going down on you earlier today, and since then, well, I haven't been able to think of much else."

My breath rushes out. "That was me. I mentioned that."

His lips quirk. "Yes, you did, love."

I grin. "And you're looking forward to that, are you? That's something you enjoy?"

"It's something I'm dying for. I intend to worship your pussy as if you were a queen and peace in the kingdom depended on your utter satisfaction."

My eyes widen. "That sounds weirdly proper. But also amazing. Let's go do that now. We can cut through the woods and be at my place in fifteen minutes. Twenty tops. And it's too early in the year for ticks so we won't have to worry about Lyme disease!"

He laughs. "I have to check on Beatrice first. I

imagine she'll be waiting with Cassie at the finish line, so…" He nods toward the cemetery. "Shall we find the place that proves love never dies and finish this? Together?"

I wrap my arms around his waist, hugging him closer. "Together. I'm not letting you out of my sight or my arms again for a very long time."

"Thank God."

9

Colin

WE FIND THE CLUE BEHIND A STATUE OF A HUSBAND AND wife holding hands across the space between their two headstones, forming a delicate bridge between them. The stone lovers gaze adoringly into each other's eyes, making mine fill with tears again as Savannah pulls the clue from a small envelope taped to the back of the larger headstone.

"The factory!" She leaps back to her feet with a triumphant pump of her fist. "The last stop is Sunshine Toys—it has to be! Where else do *frisky kitties go to feel pretty*?" She spins, and her smile falls as her gaze locks on my face. "Oh, no. Are you okay?" Her breath rushes out. "Oh my God, Colin, I'm sorry. I didn't even think. This must be hard for you. Being in a cemetery like this, by a statue like this. Does it make you miss her terribly? Cathryn?"

Hearing my former wife's name should hurt, I suppose—it always has before—but it doesn't this time.

And I'm not sad. I'm grateful. Grateful for a second chance at love and grateful that I know without a doubt that Cathryn would be glad that I've found love again.

"I'll always miss her. She was my first love, and she gave me Bea, but..." I reach out, taking Savannah's hand again. "She's happy for me. For us. I know she is. I can feel it." I glance around the peaceful graveyard, struck by the feeling that we might not be alone here, but that any spirits lingering in this tidy patch of green mean us well. "There's something magical about this town, isn't there?"

"Yes, there is," Savannah says just as a flock of geese explodes from the woods across the street.

No, not geese. It's a flock of old women. Wearing bright pink "Mama Wants Some Lovin'" tee-shirts and picking dead leaves out of their silver hair as they hustle across the quiet road. "We're almost there, ladies! First round's on me if we win! All those people who think we're too old to find true love again are going to eat their words with a pickle juice chaser."

Savannah and I lock eyes, and she smiles. "Are you thinking what I'm thinking?"

"I am. Last one to help an old lady win the hell out of this hunt is a rotten egg?"

She beams at me. "Just when I thought I couldn't love you more." Then she kisses my cheek and lifts a hand to the women hurrying through the cemetery gate. "Over here, y'all! We found it!"

And we have.

We've found it, and now that we have, I know we're never going to let it go.

TWENTY MINUTES LATER, WE JOG INTO TOWN IN THE middle of a pack of seniors and are met with cheers from the bystanders watching from either side of the drive leading up to Sunshine Toys. We left our bikes behind to pick up later, and Savannah and I have been playing the part of the woodland creatures that helped us stay at the front of the pack, aiding our crew of ladies on their quest to share the prize.

We pass Beatrice and Cassie, and Savannah stops briefly to hug them both and shout over the hubbub to Bea, "I love you and am so happy to see you! And I love your dad, too! And he loves me!"

Beatrice's jaw drops, and her eyes fill with happiness so intense it would be enough to get me down on one knee, even if I wasn't madly in love with Savannah. But I am and I am going to have to find a ring shop —ASAP.

Bea's gaze darts to my face. "Finally," she says, making me laugh. "I thought you two were never going to wake up and smell the romance."

Cassie laughs hard enough that the pair of hedge-hogs strapped to her chest—it's Happy Cat, of course—

jiggle and bounce and squeak as though they're afraid they might fall out of the sling.

We round the final corner into the parking lot, and our entire group grinds to a halt with a collective gasp.

A slender blond woman is marching Savannah's ex-husband and his new girlfriend out the factory's front doors, right beneath the large sun making a mid-orgasm face that adorns the building.

The man is pale and sweating, and his companion's wooly jacket is…smoking?

Is that smoke drifting off the jacket?

"*Olivia!*" Savannah cries.

Ah, so *this* is Savannah's best friend from childhood. But from all the stories I've heard about free-spirited, crystal-collecting Olivia, the last thing I expected when meeting her for the first time was to encounter a Viking warrioress with fury etched on her features.

"Savannah!" Oliva's eyes widen. "I just caught your ex trying to steal—*dang it!*"

Her words end in a soft growl as Steve, the dirty rat, takes advantage of her distraction to spin in a circle and grab her from behind.

"What the devil is that?" I ask Savannah and the seniors standing close by.

"Something not good," Savannah says as she breaks into a run again. I follow her, as do several of the spry older women, all of us racing toward where Steve has one arm wrapped around Olivia's throat.

With the other, he holds some sort of device to her head.

"Stop, or the mystic nutjob gets her brains fried!" he shouts.

"Oh, no, you don't, you sheep-fucker!" one of the older women yells back. "Let that sweet girl go!"

Savannah skids to a halt a few yards from her ex and throws out an arm, signaling for the rest of us to stop. "Let her go, Steve!" she orders. In a softer voice, she whispers to me over her shoulder, "It's a taser. I think that's what happened to his lady-friend's jacket. Steve has a habit of setting things on fire 'accidentally on purpose.' But I didn't know that until after we were married. I swear. I wasn't smart about living with a guy for a few years before I fell in love back then."

"I'm sick of this town and the way it worships you," Steve sneers at her. "Everyone thinks you're so special just because you were famous. You get away with murder, walking all over other people, doing whatever you want without giving a shit about anyone else. You ruined my life, you selfish bitch."

Van balls her fists and glares back at him, holding me back from leaping to tackle him. "You ruined your own life, Steve. And abused a farm animal while you were at it. And now you're, what? Threatening to zap an innocent woman's brains out? This isn't going to end well for you, dude. The best thing you can do is put the taser down and walk away."

"We should've taken care of him *my* way when we had the chance," one of the senior citizens murmurs.

"Now's not the time, Ruthie May," another mutters back. "Olivia's safety is what's important right now. And remember what we discussed about *not talking about certain plans in public,* mm-kay? Plausible deniability is going to be important when the man disappears."

Indeed. As a lawyer, I couldn't agree more. I'm appalled the American justice system allowed this madman back on the streets. Once I've passed the necessary bar exam and am cleared to practice in this country, I'll do what I can to help keep dangerous men like this behind bars where they belong.

But in the meantime…

I glance around, looking for something to use to diffuse the situation and save Savannah's friend, but there's nothing, not so much as a large stick or heavy rock. This entire area has obviously been cleared to make room for the treasure hunters and spectators.

"I'm going to *drive* away, thanks. And you don't get to tell me what to do anymore! I'm the boss of my life." Steve backs toward a car. "Get ready to drive," he tells his girlfriend, whose jacket is still slightly smoky.

She eyes him uncertainly, making me think she's the weak link in this plan.

"*I said get ready to drive,*" he snarls.

"You're doing it again, Steve," Savannah calls. "You're ruining your own life. You can't keep treating people like extras in *The Steve Show.* Oliva is a wife and a mother and a sweet person who never did anything to deserve being threatened and mistreated. Come on. Seriously, don't you want to be a better man than this? Because you still can be. You can choose to be better!"

"And you can choose something better, as well," I urge his girlfriend, catching and holding her trouble gaze. "Do you really want to align yourself with a man who'd happily see you incarcerated as his accomplice in crime?"

"*Shut up!*" Steve screeches, his face turning red.

"No, Steve, *you shut up!*" Olivia shouts. "And say hello to my little friend."

She swings an elbow into his gut at the same time that mischievous raccoon leaps from the overhang above the factory entrance, landing on Steve's head, scratching and slapping at his cheeks while chittering something that sounds like a scolding I used to get from my mother.

Olivia darts away as Steve spins, trying to shoot the raccoon with the taser. But the half-plucked goose joins the fray then, charging forward with a vicious honk as it aims its beak at his family jewels.

The goose hits its target, Steve drops the taser, the raccoon grabs it, and then—

Steve makes a shocked, gargling noise and drops like a sack of potatoes.

"*Olivia,*" Savannah cries again, dashing to snatch her friend up in a hug.

"*Savannah!* Oh, you're home! I missed you! And— look at you! *Look at you!* Your aura is glowing! You've found love again, haven't you? I can't wait to hear all about it! Tell me everything!"

I gape at the two women and point to Steve's

twitching form on the ground. "That man was holding you hostage."

"But I wasn't alone this time, and I wasn't in that horrible clown school, and I knew I'd be okay." Olivia beams at me as though all of that makes perfect sense. "You must be Colin. Your aura has the same glow as Savannah's. Oh, you two are just the cutest! I'm so glad to meet you! Welcome to Happy Cat!"

"The prize!" one of the ladies yells, motioning for the others to follow her into the factory as two familiar men come rushing in to tie up Steve, with the help of a third man in a fire department shirt and uniform pants.

"Can I punch him?" the firefighter asks.

"After me," the man I now recognize as Jace replies.

"Hey. Don't mess him up too badly. He has to be recognizable in his mugshot. No technicalities this time around," Blake says. "Especially while he's still half-unconscious. The sheriff's on his way. We need this to go down right."

"Can George *please* get a medal for his bravery this time?" Olivia calls to them.

Jace goes moon-eyed. "Anything for you, my angel."

She beams.

Savannah slips to my side and tucks her hand into mine, the simple squeeze of her fingers doing more to assure me that the danger has truly passed than anything else. "So, this is Happy Cat," she says with a smile. "Maybe we should do a trial period to make sure you'll be comfortable here? We're weird. Fun, good weird, mostly, but weird."

"Papa!" Bea races up to us and hugs us both. She's nearly as tall as Savannah these days, and as I wrap my arms around both of them, I feel something I haven't felt in too long.

Complete.

"It's all right," I tell my daughter. "Everyone's safe now."

"George is so brave," Bea says, awe in her tone.

"He really is," Savannah agrees. "My favorite fat, fluffy superhero."

"Mine too. Cassie invited me to have a bunking party with George and his family tonight." Bea smiles at me with the same mischievous energy as the raccoon who's waddling over to join Cassie, the hedgehogs, and two toddlers—one boy, one girl—whose hands she's now holding. "May I, Papa? I promise I'll behave."

Savannah squeezes my waist. "I think that sounds like amazing fun."

"And then you can treat Savannah to a proper date," Bea adds with a wink. "Girls like proper dates."

"Are you conspiring, my sweet child?" I ask her.

Her grin is all the answer I need.

I love Savannah. Beatrice loves Savannah. Savannah loves us.

And now Savannah's ex-husband is headed back to prison, helped along by a sheriff's deputy who's just arrived on the scene.

The "Mama Wants Some Lovin'" team of senior citizens emerge from the factory a few moments later, and together they hold aloft the prize, which appears to be some kind of medal.

"Beatrice, Logan, and Clover are about due for an afternoon snack," Cassie says. "Would you like to join us?"

"Oh, yes, Colin, do join us!" Olivia slides over beside us again. This time, Jace is with her, carrying the little girl previously tagging along with Cassie. "I would *love* to get to know you better."

Jace eyes me, then Savannah, and then me again. "Me too, assuming I'll never have to tie you up with fuzzy handcuffs I borrowed from an adult toy factory while chasing away a woman who dresses like a sheep. You're not going to make me do that, right?"

My eyeballs bulge. "Dear God, no."

He nods once, then smirks. "Good. Welcome to Happy Cat."

"Ignore Mr. Moody," the man in the firefighter uniform says as he swoops up the smaller toddler. "We're glad to have you, Colin. Cassie's told us all about you. You're quite the regular topic of conversation between my wife and Van."

"Can we please save ambushing my poor Colin until after we've both recovered from jetlag?" Savannah interrupts. She yawns, loud and long. "I'm so tired. I need a nap. Don't you, Colin?"

"Yes," I answer without hesitation. "A very, very long nap."

"I hate naps," Beatrice mutters.

"You might not when you're older," Cassie says with a wink.

The adults all laugh.

Except me.

And Savannah.

We lock eyes, and I know what she wants.

She wants *me*.

And I am officially the happiest man on earth.

10

Colin

Savannah's home is as whimsical, bright, and beautiful as she is, but I don't spare the décor more than a glance. I'm too focused on the gorgeous woman pulling me through the door and kissing me with enough heat to set ten sheep coats on fire.

"You're sure you don't mind leaving your prize behind?" I murmur as I lift her into my arms.

Her legs go around my waist. "I have my prize right here," she whispers against my lips. "And I can't wait to attend five senior weddings later this year. Those ladies know how to tear it up on the dance floor."

"I want to dance with you." I dig my fingers into her hips through her soft leggings. "I want to do everything with you."

"Yes, please," she says between kisses. "The

bedroom is that way. Please go that way. As fast as you possibly can."

I break into a run that makes her giggle and screech, "Too fast, too fast!" She's still laughing as I toss her on a big, fluffy white bed, but her smile fades as I reach for the top button on my shirt.

Her tongue slips out to dampen her lips, and a hungry sound vibrates low in her throat. "I can't decide if I want you to go fast so I can finally see you naked or slow to draw out the excitement even more."

"How about both?" I move my fingers quickly down the row of buttons as I toe off my shoes and socks. "Fast first because I can't wait to touch you. Then as slow and seductive as you'd like the next time around. I'll even do a striptease if you'd like."

"Oh, I would like. My stuffy, sugar-free Colin bumping and grinding for me sounds delicious."

"Only for you, love." I shove my pants to the floor and crawl up to join her on the bed in nothing but my boxer briefs. She sighs as I lengthen myself on top of her, and my heart nearly bursts from my chest.

"I can't believe this is real," I confess. "I've dreamt about this so many times, and now…you're finally here. Finally mine."

"Yes. *Yes*. I'm all yours." She strokes my erection through the thin cotton. "And I want to be yours even more, in every way. I love you so much. Let's always love each other and never hurt each other and live happily ever after, okay?"

"I'll never hurt you, sweetheart," I say, kissing her

softly this time. This kiss is a promise, a vow. "I will fight for you and laugh with you and make big, beautiful plans with you, and I will never do a single thing to dim your light or break your heart."

Her eyes are shining as she cradles my face. "Same, my love. I promise." She sniffs, collecting herself as she adds with a mischievous smile, "But if you want to break my pussy a little, I don't mind. I like it a little frisky, if you know what I mean."

I thread my fingers into the hair at the nape of her neck and make a fist, tugging her head gently backward, loving the way her breath rushes out in response. "Like this?"

"Oh, yes," she says, her voice thick with the same longing hammering through my veins. "Dear God, you're even more perfect than I thought."

Grinning, I drop my lips to her throat, kissing her as I murmur against her soft flesh, "Oh, darling, you haven't seen anything yet. I promise."

And then I proceed to keep that promise, one kiss at a time.

Savannah

I'M A SEXUALLY LIBERATED WOMAN.

I love sex, I embrace pleasure, and I thought I knew a thing or two about a thing or two.

But soon, Colin has stripped me of my clothes and my preconceived notions, and I realize I knew nothing. Absolutely nothing.

"Oh my God," I shout again. I've shouted it at least four or five times already, but I can't stop myself, not while Colin's rolling his tongue against my clit as his elegant, oh-so-capable fingers thrust and beckon inside me, swiftly bringing me back to precipice all over again. "Oh, yes, yes!"

I come with my heels digging into the mattress, pressing my sex shamelessly against his talented face, but he doesn't seem to mind. In fact, judging by the hungry groan that rumbles from his chest, he's loving this every bit as much as I am.

But I need more of him, all of him.

"You. Now. Please," I beg, clawing at his bare shoulders.

A beat later, his lips are on mine and the thick, fever-hot head of his cock is brushing against my thigh as he breathes, "Condom. Fuck. I think I have one in my luggage in the car. I haven't had sex in so long I'm positive I'm clean, but—"

"Me, too. No condom," I say, wrapping my legs around his waist. "I'm not on birth control, but the doctors were firm that I can't..."

"Savannah, I love you exactly as you are, and I intend to help you learn to love yourself exactly as you are too. No what-ifs. No regrets."

My heart blossoms brightly inside my chest at just how much this man loves me. I arch upward, doing my best to wiggle him inside me, but he grips my hips and pins me to the mattress in a way that does nothing to cool the fire burning inside of me.

"I want to experience all of our joys and heartbreaks together from now on," he says in a husky voice that goes straight to my heart. And my pussy. "I never want you to get bad news alone again. I want to be there for you when you need me, for whatever you need me for. I want to marry you, Savannah, and live out my dreams with you for the rest of my life."

"Then marry me. Tomorrow morning if you like," I say, raking my nails down his back to grip his ass. "But make love to me first, please. I need dick."

"You need *my* dick, you mean," he says, nearly making me swoon again.

Hearing him use such enticing, erotic words will never get old. I shiver as he nips at my throat and releases my hips. "Yes, and I need you to say crass things like 'dick' and 'fuck' as often as possible while we're naked, please."

"How about I tell you that I'm going to fuck this sweet pussy until she comes hard on my fat dick? Is that—"

His words end in a moan as I kiss him hard, deep, and hungry. And then his fat, delicious cock is gliding into where I'm so wet and ready for him, and I'm in paradise.

This is it. Paradise. Nirvana.

The sweetest feeling of sexy rightness I've ever known.

"I'll never use a vibrator again," I pant as he rides me hard, and I cling to him, meeting him thrust for thrust. "No silicone could ever compare to this perfect cock. I'm in love with it. And you. And life. And oh God… Oh God, Colin!"

I come so hard that I have an out-of-body experience. I'm only dimly aware of Colin's cry of release and the wonderful way he twitches inside me, and when we've caught our breath a few minutes later, I can't help feeling a little sad about it.

"What's wrong, love?" he asks, brushing my hair from my sweat-dampened forehead.

"I didn't get to appreciate your orgasm as much as I wanted to." I stare at him helplessly. "I was too distracted by mine."

He chuckles. "It's all right. I have a feeling we'll get another shot at coming, both separately and together." He gives me an unexpectedly saucy wink as he adds, "We really are frightfully good at fucking, aren't we? Especially considering it was our first time."

I will never get enough of my dear, perfect Colin, and I can't stop touching him and marveling at his body either. "Nothing frightening about it. Assuming you can get it up again in say…three minutes."

"How about one?" He guides my hand to where he is indeed rallying with incredible speed.

I sigh. "Yes. That's my man. That's my glorious, lovely man."

And he is both of those things, a fact he proves several times that night and again the next morning.

WE'RE MARRIED THREE DAYS LATER IN A SIMPLE CEREMONY in the town square—it took more time to get a license than we thought—and Colin gives notice at the Government Legal Service and sends for his and Beatrice's things the day after. We move into my home together, Beatrice has bunking parties with George every weekend, and fifteen months later, I get a call from the adoption agency that the birth mother who chose our family for her baby has gone into labor.

Six hours later, I'm holding my baby girl, Sarah, my second daughter, my heart.

Swiping tears from my eyes, I look up at Colin in the maternity ward waiting room and whisper, "Again. Let's do it again."

He smiles and kisses my forehead, his own emotions reverberating in his voice. "I never took our name off the list with the other agency. I had a feeling we'd want to go big with this whole family thing."

"I love you," I say, still sniffling. "And I love our girls. I can't believe this is my life."

I can't, not for a long time. It's just too good, too happy, too full of love and laughter and simple, everyday joy.

But by the time baby Nate is settled in my arms just a few weeks after Sarah's first birthday, I'm starting to get the hang of this happily ever after thing.

And it's flat-out awesome. Five out of five stars. Would highly recommend.

EPILOGUE

Twitch the British Bunny, aka a hideaway in a Happy Cat backyard

My humans are frolicking again.

Well, they don't know they're my humans, but *I* know they are, and I love watching the sisters and brother play.

I've even acquired an accent like the eldest girl after listening to her read aloud to the younger ones and eavesdropping on her lessons on how to speak proper English. If it's proper, then I intend to embrace every bit of it. I may be an orphan who was washed from my burrow as a babe and grew up wild and rangy in the woods, but I'm clever and good with a turn of phrase, if I do say so myself.

"Now, Sarah, if you want to say you're happy, you

say you're *chuffed*. Isn't that so much more lovely than psyched or stoked?"

Chuffed, I whisper to myself. I'm *chuffed* to have a family of humans, even if they don't know they're my family or realize I live in a hole beneath the treehouse where they gather to have their secret meetings.

"Chuffed," a much younger voice says, and then a younger-still voice attempts to say it as well. *"Hupped."*

"Very good, Nate! You're getting it now!"

The two smallest humans were already walking by the time I found my way to this safe refuge from the foxes and coyotes and the other predators roaming the woods, but the youngest still isn't quite steady on his feet. He has to have help getting up into the treehouse, and his biggest sister always carries him carefully down again.

She is truly a treasure. If I could choose any human to be my special friend, it would be her. I imagine she would tell me wonderful bedtime stories and pet me every bit as carefully as she tends to her little siblings.

"Isn't that brilliant, Sarah?" Beatrice asks. She's the eldest, and I adore her name. It's so lovely. "You could barely talk at all when you were his age."

"'Cause he's a wanker!" comes the enthusiastic reply from the smaller girl.

"Sarah! No, no, we never call people wankers!"

"But Papa says *wanker*."

"Well, Papa isn't perfect," Beatrice says. "Close, but not quite."

I sniff the air for danger and inch closer to the discussion.

This sounds almost as juicy as the spinach leaves growing in the garden on the other side of the yard.

"What are you doing?" a raccoon chitters at me, materializing from behind a nearby bush like a chubby, and slightly scary, ghost.

I leap in fright, torn between dashing back to my hole and staying still to trick the raccoon into thinking I'm a statue. This is an excellent self-defense strategy, as long as the predator in question isn't very smart. Or terribly hungry.

"Relax, bun-bun. Nobody's gonna hurt you. Except maybe Lucifer, the cat. He's a good egg, but Cassie put him on a diet, so best to steer clear of him for the foreseeable future." The raccoon chuckles. "I'm George. What's your name?"

I remain still, torn and a little suspicious. Raccoons aren't as chompy as other animals that eat bunnies, but they will sink a tooth into you if given the chance.

"C'mon, cottontail," he chitters. "Sticky Fingers and I have been watching you. We know you've been nibbling in Savannah and Colin's garden. We know you could use a friend. And *I* know how you can get fed for a lot less work."

"Is this a trap?" I ask him.

His eyes widen as he sits back on his fluffy backside. "An English bunny? How'd that happen? Did you stow away in the big guy's luggage?"

"Something like that," I answer vaguely.

"Well, in any event, we neighborhood animals stick together around here," he replies solemnly. "And you're one of us now. Let me help you out, kid. You seem a little twitchy."

"That's my name. Twitch."

George grunts. "That makes a lot of sense, Twitch. Why don't you come with me, buddy? Let me help you find a home?"

My nose quivers in excitement, and my ears twitch faster. Even my tail is vibrating. "Really? You really want to help me…and be my friend?"

"Friend and mentor. One day, we'll need new animals to watch out for the people of Happy Cat, and you look like the kind of bunny who might be up for the job." He jerks his head toward the house with my humans. "Follow me. I know how to get inside."

I lift my eyes to the treehouse again, where Beatrice is explaining something called *spotted dick* to the younger two.

"But will they want me?" I ask George, uncertainty rising inside of me again. "No one has ever wanted me before. Once I was washed from my burrow as a baby, none of the other rabbits wanted me in their family."

"I'm sorry about that, kid. Forest animals can be brutal sometimes." He rests a gentle paw on my back, which makes me twitch harder for a moment before I realize he doesn't mean me harm. His paw is gentle, nice even. "But these people will love you, I swear, trash panda's honor. And you're gonna love them. And those two little guys up there? They're adopted too."

The news makes my heart leap, and my ears perk up.

George grins. "See? This is going to be great. Just wait and see. C'mon, Twitch. Let me introduce you to your new family."

And that's exactly what he does.

I won't give you all the details—there was a lot of screaming involved at first and some worries about rabies and whether I might secretly be a ninja—but now?

Now, I sleep with Beatrice every night, and she feeds me carrots every morning. We play with her siblings in the backyard after she comes home from school and have more fun than I imagined possible when I was a lonely orphan bunny without a place to call my own.

Now, I have a human family and an animal family, and I am chuffed about it.

Absolutely, positively chuffed.

The Complete Happy Cat Series
Hosed (Ryan & Cassie)
Hammered (Jace & Olivia)
Hitched (Blake & Hope)
Humbugged (Clint & Noelle)
Happily Ever Aftered (Colin & Savannah)

www.ingramcontent.com/pod-product-compliance
Lightning Source LLC
Chambersburg PA
CBHW021722190726
48289CB00008B/2652